The Boxcar Children Mysteries

W9-BMN-442

THE MYSTERY OF THE SCREECH OWL

created by
GERTRUDE CHANDLER WARNER

Illustrated by Hodges Soileau

ALBERT WHITMAN & Company
Chicago, Illinois

Activities by Kimberly Weinberger
Activity illustrations by Alfred Giuliani

No part of this publication may be reproduced, or stored in a retrieval system, or transmitted in any form, or by any means, electronic, mechanical, photo-copying, recording, or otherwise, without written permission of the publisher. For information regarding permission, write to Albert Whitman & Company.

ISBN 978-0-8075-5482-1

Copyright © 2001 by Albert Whitman & Company. All rights reserved. BOXCAR CHILDREN is a registered trademark of Albert Whitman & Company.

10 9 8 7 6 5 4 3 2 LB 15 14 13 12 11 10

Printed in the U.S.A.

Contents

Contents

CHAPTER 1

Broken Moon Pond

"Snow!" exclaimed Jessie Alden, peering out the rental car window. "When we left Greenfield this morning, Mrs. McGregor's daffodils were blooming."

"Canada is farther north. It snows even in the spring here," said Henry from the front seat. At fourteen, he knew a lot about the places the Alden family visited.

"Fun!" said six-year-old Benny. He was thrilled to see snow any time of the year.

"I can't wait to see Broken Moon Pond,"

said Violet, sitting beside Benny. "It sounds great."

Grandfather slowed down for a curve in the country road. "I can't wait to see it, either," he replied. "I haven't been there since I was ten years old."

"You were my age," Violet remarked, gazing at the passing scenery of patchy snow and stark trees.

"We came every year at this time," Grandfather went on. "My parents were friends of the Dupré family, who own Broken Moon Pond. In those days, we didn't fly from Connecticut to Quebec and rent a car. It took much longer to get here."

"Did you come by horse and buggy?" asked Benny.

Everyone laughed.

Jessie reached across the seat to ruffle her little brother's hair. "Benny, Grandfather isn't *that* old!" At twelve, Jessie liked to look after her younger brother.

After their parents died, the Alden children lived in an abandoned boxcar. They learned to take care of themselves because they believed they were alone in the world.

But their grandfather, James Alden, found the children and gave them a real home. The children were happy living in Greenfield with Mrs. McGregor, the housekeeper, and Watch, their dog. Grandfather even had their old boxcar towed to the backyard so they could play in it.

Now they were off on a late-spring trip to Broken Moon Pond.

"There's the sign to Nibelle," Henry pointed out. He sat up front to give directions.

Grandfather turned off onto another road. Moments later, trees and fields gave way to farmhouses and then the village of Nibelle.

Old stone buildings were arranged around a square with a fountain in the middle. Grandfather pulled the car into a parking spot.

"This is the real estate agent's office," he said. "I need to pick up the key to our cabin."

"Doesn't the Dupré family live there?"

asked Jessie as she got out and stretched.

Grandfather put on his wool hat. "I don't know. When I phoned the main cabin, my call was switched to this agency. Let's go in and we'll find out."

The air was chilly. Violet hurried into the stone building after Benny. Inside, she squinted in the dim interior.

"*Bonjour,*" said a voice from the gloom. A man rose from behind a desk. When he saw the Aldens, the smile dropped from his face.

"I'm James Alden," said Grandfather. "You are expecting us."

In accented English, the man said stiffly, "My name is Monsieur Cartier. How may I help you?"

"We are renting a cabin at Broken Moon Pond this week," said Grandfather. "And we are here to pick up the key."

"*Oui,*" said Mr. Cartier. "*Une seconde.*" He went into another room.

Benny frowned. "What kind of talk is that?"

"He's speaking French," said Henry. "Re-member the lady on the loudspeaker system in the Quebec airport? She spoke French. That's the main language here."

"Will we have to speak French, too?" Benny asked, concerned. "I don't know how."

"I brought a French-English dictionary," Jessie said. "We can look up words we don't understand. And Grandfather speaks a little."

Just then Mr. Cartier came back. He held up a key ring. "I am sorry I was so long. My assistant is away and I cannot find anything."

"Are the Duprés here?" Grandfather asked.

Mr. Cartier shook his head. "Only a few Dupré family members remain and they no longer come to the pond. They rent out the cabins to tourists. As a matter of fact, the estate is up for sale."

"Broken Moon Pond is for sale?" Grandfather echoed, surprised. "That property has been in the family for generations."

Mr. Cartier shrugged. "No one comes now. And it is a difficult property to sell. It is a — how do you say — a white elephant."

In the car, Grandfather said, "I still can't believe the pond is for sale. And the place is hardly a white elephant."

"Is there a white elephant where we're going?" Benny asked hopefully.

"That's an expression," said Henry. "It means a house or a place that is too big or odd for anyone to want to buy."

They drove out of Nibelle. Benny noticed a couple of men putting up a bright yellow banner across the narrow street.

"What does that say?" he asked.

"It's about the sugar festival," Grandfather replied. "This is sugaring season. The villagers make maple syrup. Then they have a festival."

"Just for syrup? I'm going to like it here!" Benny exclaimed, licking his lips. He loved to eat. Any place that celebrated making sugar was definitely where Benny wanted to be.

It didn't take them long to reach Broken Moon Pond. Jessie thought she had never seen such a beautiful spot.

Evergreen trees towered over a huge pond, reflecting dark shapes. Rustic log cabins ringed the pond and a large dock jutted halfway across the still water.

Grandfather pulled the car into the driveway of the largest cabin.

"This is the main house," he said. "The Duprés built this camp many years ago. They had a big family. Everyone spent the summer here and they'd bring their children and friends. That's why there are so many cabins. When we visited, we stayed in the main cabin."

"All out!" Henry called. He opened the trunk and began setting suitcases on the snow-covered ground.

Benny ran up the steps and onto the porch that spanned the front of the house. Whole logs had been used as posts.

"Look what I found!" he exclaimed. "Skates! And funny-looking things to put on our feet!" He held up a pair of snowshoes.

"Those are for walking in deep snow," Grandfather said, bringing up the first load

of luggage. "We won't need those unless we have a storm, which could happen even at this time of year."

Taking out the key ring, he tried the key. It didn't work. Jiggling the lock, he tried again.

"The key doesn't fit," he said. Just to make sure, he tried all the keys on the ring. None of them opened the door. "I bet Mr. Cartier gave me the wrong key ring."

Jessie thumped her suitcase on the porch. "Now what?"

"I'll drive back to the village and pick up the right keys," said Grandfather. "Hop in the car again, everybody."

At that moment, four children appeared at the bottom of the steps.

"Hi," said the oldest, a girl about Henry's age. "I'm Patty Anderson. These are my brothers, Aaron and Jacob, and my little sister, Emma." Emma was just a toddler, but she smiled at the Aldens.

"Nice to meet you," said Henry. He introduced Benny, Violet, Jessie, and Grandfather. "We just got here, but our key doesn't fit. We're going back to Nibelle."

"Oh, why don't you stay here," Patty urged. "We're in the cabin across the pond with my mom and dad."

"I'll only be gone fifteen minutes," Grandfather said to the kids. "It's okay if you want to stay."

The Aldens and Andersons strolled around the pond.

"This is such a great place," said Aaron, who was Jessie's age.

"It looks neat," Henry agreed.

"There's our dad," said Jacob, waving to a man who was walking down to the pond with a tackle box and fishing pole.

"Hi, neighbors," Mr. Anderson greeted them. "Isn't it nice that there are two families here with four kids?"

"Are we the only people here?" asked Benny.

"Most people come when the weather is warmer," said Mr. Anderson. "But we like it here any time of the year."

"Wait until you taste the food they have here," said Aaron. "Yum!"

"The caretaker and his wife live in the village, but they left us supper," Patty explained. "And there's some in the refrigerator for you, too."

Henry looked out across the water. "I see Grandfather's car. We'd better go. See you later!"

The Andersons called good-bye as the Alden children ran up the stone path to the main cabin.

Grandfather already had the door open and was taking their luggage inside. "Mr. Cartier was very apologetic," he said. "I have a feeling his assistant really runs that office!"

Violet helped carry in the rest of the bags. Then she stopped to look around.

Bright wool blankets hung on the exposed log walls. Even the furniture was made of logs and saplings. An enormous stone fireplace took up one end of the living room. Above, a real birchbark canoe was suspended from the high-beamed ceiling. Lightbulbs edged the rim of the canoe.

"Let's pick out our bedrooms," said Jessie.

The second story had been divided into dormitories, one for girls, one for boys. Grandfather was sleeping in one of the downstairs bedrooms.

The girls chose a room overlooking the pond and picnic area. Henry and Benny decided on a room decorated with old boating flags.

"Supper!" Grandfather called.

The kids ran downstairs. They didn't need to be called twice, especially Benny.

"Mmmm," Violet said, smelling something wonderful. "What's for dinner?"

Grandfather carried a dish to the table. "The caretaker's wife left us a meat pie and *tarte du sucre* for dessert."

"Tart *what*?" asked Benny.

"Maple sugar pie," answered Grandfather.

Two kinds of pie for dinner! Benny liked this place more and more. The meat pie was hearty and the maple sugar pie was so good, everyone ate seconds.

When the dishes were washed, the kids went back upstairs to unpack.

Jessie claimed the old dresser by the window, while Violet took the rickety wardrobe.

"This drawer is really stuck," said Jessie, tugging on a small drawer at the top. "I guess it's the damp air."

With a jerk, she yanked the drawer backward. As she did, something dropped at her feet.

"What's that?" asked Violet.

As Jessie bent to pick up the object, it opened. "I've never seen anything like this before!" she said with wonder.

CHAPTER 2

CHAPTER 2

The Mysterious Notebook

At that moment, someone rapped at the door.

Henry poked his head in. "We saw your light still on," he said. "Everything okay?"

Benny came in behind Henry. He noticed the object in Jessie's hand. "What's that?"

"It's a book. It was jammed in the back of the drawer," Jessie replied. "But it's not like any book I've ever seen before."

Carefully, she opened the cracked leather covers. The others gathered around.

The paper was old and yellowed. The

14

first page showed a sketch of a deer. In the upper corners were drawings of the deer's head in different poses, chewing grass, listening, and drinking water. Neat writing in English and another language framed the sketches.

"Whoever drew this was a good artist," Violet remarked. She was an artist herself and often drew and painted pictures.

"I like this one," said Benny when Jessie turned to the next page. "The grasshopper looks real. But what does that writing say?"

"The English part says where the grasshopper was found and how big it was," Henry replied. "I don't know what the French part says. The person who kept this notebook could write in both English and French."

"He — or she — must have been pretty smart," said Jessie.

"It's fairly common in this part of Canada to speak both languages," Henry said. He took the notebook and flipped through pages of drawings. "You know what this is? It's a field journal."

"What's that?" asked Violet.

"Scientists who study nature keep records of the birds and animals and insects they see," answered Henry. "But these drawings were done by a kid."

Jessie wiped dust from the worn leather cover. "Whoever it was kept the notebook a long time ago. It's pretty old."

Benny yawned. Tired, he lost interest in the old journal. "We'd better get to bed, Henry. I want to go exploring first thing in the morning."

"Before breakfast?" Violet teased.

"Not *that* early," said Benny, who never missed a meal.

The boys said good night and went across the hall to their own room.

Jessie and Violet finished unpacking. Jessie left the field journal on the dresser. When she switched off the lamp, moonlight filled the narrow room.

"It's as bright as day in here," said Violet. She walked over to the big window to pull the shade.

Screee! Shrieeek!

"What was *that*?" Jessie exclaimed, rushing to the window.

"I don't know," said Violet. "I've never heard anything like it."

The moon was reflected in the pond like a silver dollar. Something ruffled the surface, causing the reflection to waver and break.

"Now I know how the pond got its name," Jessie murmured. "But what was that horrible sound?"

Violet tensed. "Jessie, look over there. By the dock."

From the shadow of the dock an object glided across the water. It was a rowboat. *Who would be out rowing in the dark?* Jessie wondered.

Violet clutched her sleeve.

"Jessie!" she whispered. "*Nobody* is rowing that boat!"

Jessie looked again. Was it a trick of the moonlight or was the boat actually rowing itself across the pond?

The boat slid around to the other side of the dock, disappearing from sight. Jessie blinked, but the boat was gone.

"We must be very tired," she told Violet. "Maybe the wind pushed the boat away from the dock."

"There's no wind," Violet observed. "The water is as still as glass. Nothing moved on that pond but the boat. A boat rowed by no one!"

The girls went back to bed.

Jessie had trouble falling asleep. She kept picturing the empty boat moving across the dark water. Violet was right — they hadn't imagined what they had just seen. At last, she fell asleep.

The next morning, the smell of fried potatoes and sizzling bacon drifted upstairs. The Alden children dressed hurriedly and ran down to the big open kitchen.

Grandfather stood at the old-fashioned stove, expertly flipping flapjacks onto a cast-iron griddle.

"I thought you kids were going to sleep

all day," he said, teasing. "But I figured out a way to get you up."

Benny carried the jug of warm maple syrup over to the polished oak table. "I'm starving," he exclaimed. "Grandfather, may I have a dozen pancakes?"

Violet laughed. "When aren't you starving, Benny Alden? And I don't think even you can eat a dozen of Grandfather's pancakes."

Crispy bacon, home fries, and cold milk rounded out the hearty meal. James Alden's famous pancakes were so huge, even Henry couldn't eat a dozen, but everyone gave it a try.

"There's frost on the windows," Jessie observed. "That means it's really cold. Will it snow?"

"It could, but the weather report on the radio said it would be sunny today," said Grandfather. "At least, that's what I *think* the radio announcer said. The broadcast was in French."

"Then we can go exploring," Benny said.

"Of course," Grandfather said. "Just wear

your coats and hats. These cold nights and warm days are perfect conditions for the sap to rise in the sugar bush."

Everyone looked puzzled. Grandfather laughed.

"I'll take you to the sugar bush this afternoon," he said. "And you'll see what I'm talking about."

After washing the dishes, the children bundled up in jackets, scarves, and hats.

As they walked down to the edge of the pond, Violet told the boys about the boat she and Jessie had seen the night before.

"A boat with nobody rowing it?" Benny exclaimed. "How could that happen? You don't think there are any ghosts here, do you?"

"I'm sure there's a logical explanation," said Henry. "Let's look for the boat."

Now that it was bright daylight, Jessie could see the camp wore signs of neglect. The cabins around the pond were run-down. The gravel paths sprouted weeds and the lawns had gone to seed.

Down by the pond, cattails and reeds grew thickly along the shore.

They walked out on the sagging dock, carefully stepping over missing planks.

"We saw the boat leave on this side." Violet pointed. "And then it went around over here. I think I see it!"

The children hurried back down the dock, then pushed through a thicket of cattails along the shore.

A rickety rowboat was beached on the muddy bank, hidden by reeds. It had been painted dark green at one time, but the boards were mostly scraped bare. Ghostly orange letters spelled out the boat's name.

"Is this the boat?" Henry asked.

Jessie stared at it. "I think so. What's that written on the side? The letters are so faded . . . *Orville*?"

"What a funny name for a boat," Benny commented.

Henry shook his head. "Are you sure this is the boat? This old thing would sink if you tried to float it in the bathtub!"

"Well, it was night, so we couldn't see what color it was," Jessie said doubtfully. "But it *looks* like the same boat."

Just then they heard laughter and voices on the hill above them.

"The Andersons are out early, too," said Jessie, waving.

"Let's go meet them!" Benny was already halfway up the path.

Patty, Aaron, and Jacob ran the rest of the way down the hill when they saw the Aldens.

"Hi!" said Patty, her blue eyes bright with excitement. "Guess what? We're going to buy this place!"

"You're kidding!" Jessie remarked. "You're going to buy Broken Moon Pond?"

"Yep." Aaron grinned. "We like it here so much, our folks decided to buy it."

"We're going to use the cabin you're in," added Patty. "And rent out the others. After we fix them up."

"My dad called the caretaker," said Aaron. "He said we wanted to make an offer. The caretaker called the real estate man in town. We're going to see him now."

"He's the man we picked up our keys from," Jessie said, nodding. "That's **great** news."

"We saw you guys staring at something by the pond," said Aaron. "What were you looking at?"

"Just an old boat," said Benny. "We'll show you."

They went back over to the dock.

"Well?" said Patty. "I don't see anything."

Henry pushed the reeds aside. "Right there — " he began.

But there was nothing hidden among the reeds.

The boat was gone.

CHAPTER 3

The Sugar Bush

"It was right here!" cried Jessie. "An old green boat with *Orville* painted on the side."

Patty looked dubious. "Maybe the boat was someplace else and you thought it was here. These reeds are pretty thick."

"No, it was here," Henry insisted. "We all saw it. See the broken cattails?" That gave him an idea. "If the boat had been here, there would be marks in the mud."

But before he could look further, Mrs.

Anderson appeared at the top of the hill. She was carrying little Emma.

"Kids!" she called. "We're leaving!"

"We've got to go," said Aaron. "We're going to town to buy the camp!"

After the Andersons left, the Alden children searched for the vanished rowboat.

"This is too weird," said Violet, her shoes squishing as they walked back to the cabin. "How could a boat disappear?"

"And without us seeing anybody," Jessie added. She rubbed mud off her shoes on a patch of grass. "Who could have taken the boat?"

"Maybe the same person who rowed it across the pond last night," said Benny.

"But we didn't see anybody." Violet stopped. She could guess what Benny was thinking. "Benny, there are no ghosts at Broken Moon Pond." At least, she didn't *think* there were.

At that moment, Grandfather came out on the porch. "Ready for our trip?"

The children raced one another to the top of the hill.

"Where are we going?" Benny wanted to know as he fastened his seat belt in the rental car.

"Sugar bush country," was all James Alden would say.

They drove the short distance to Nibelle, then took a crooked road leading away from the village.

Deep woods surrounded the road. More snow lay on the ground. Because of the heavy forest, the sun didn't melt the snow as quickly.

A sign in French stood next to a rutted lane. Grandfather turned down the lane and stopped at a small shack. A big man in a flannel shirt leaned out the window of the shack.

"*Bonjour*," Grandfather greeted him.

"*Bonjour*," the man grunted.

Jessie whispered to Benny, "That means, 'Hello.'" She had looked up the word in her French-English dictionary.

Now James Alden was asking if they were permitted to visit the sugar bush and if there was a fee.

The man, whose name tag read ANDRÉ PLESSIS, peered into the car. He stared at the children, then said, "You are a family of four children?" He looked puzzled.

Grandfather smiled. "I am lucky enough to have four grandchildren."

"That way," André Plessis said, giving Grandfather a brochure.

Henry poked Jessie. "I wonder why that guy looks so confused."

"It's like he was expecting some other people or something," she whispered back.

They drove through the gate. Benny was the first to notice something odd about the trees.

"They have buckets on them!" he exclaimed.

"And faucets!" Violet chimed in.

Grandfather laughed at their amazement. "That's how they get sap from maple trees."

Grandfather pulled the car into a graveled lot near a long, low building and they got out.

"Mmmmm!" said Benny, taking a deep breath. "It smells like candy!"

The air does smell wonderful, Jessie thought. It made her want to eat breakfast again!

"This is the sugar hut," explained James Alden. "It's where the sap is processed into maple syrup. When I came here years ago, the hut really was a hut. Now it's a modern facility."

A tour guide met them at the door. Her name tag read MARIE-LOUISE. Jessie thought Marie-Louise was very pretty, with her long red hair and green eyes.

Marie-Louise spoke very good English. "Welcome to *cabane du sucre,* or sugar hut, as you would say. Some syrup operations use tubes to collect the sap from the trees, but here in Nibelle, we still use buckets. I will show you."

Outside again, she walked over to a large tree that had a bucket hanging from the trunk.

"The best trees are sugar maples or black maples," she explained. "Sap starts to run when the temperature is above freezing for a few days but still cold at night. We've had very good weather this year."

"Do you just stick that thing in the tree and turn it on like a faucet?" Violet asked.

"Almost," Marie-Louise replied with a smile. "First, we drill a small hole into the tree. It does not harm the tree, by the way. These trees have been tapped year after year. Next we drive in a spile, which allows the sap to flow through the spout on the end. The bucket hangs from this hook and the sap drips into it."

Henry looked around. "Do you have to carry all the buckets back to the building?"

"No," said Marie-Louise. "We collect the sap in a gathering tank and drive back to the *cabane*. But the sap must be processed immediately. That is why our operation runs day and night during sugaring season."

She led the way back to the facility. Inside, people worked over metal tubs, checking thermometers that they dipped into the vats.

Marie-Louise walked over to one of the tubs. "This is an evaporator," she said, lifting the lid. "The lid keeps the syrup clean.

This pipe carries the steam outside. That is why a sugar camp smells so good!"

"How does the sap turn into syrup?" asked Jessie.

"The evaporator boils away the water," explained Marie-Louise. "See the channels at the bottom of the pan? They allow the sap to move up and down, which concentrates the syrup."

"How long does it take?" Grandfather wanted to know. "I worked here when I was a boy, but the operations weren't modernized."

"Generally, it takes a few hours to reach sugar stage," Marie-Louise replied. "When the temperature reaches 218 degrees, the syrup is ready. But very quickly, the syrup can burn, so timing is critical."

"Grandfather, I didn't know you made syrup," said Violet.

He winked at her. "I've had a lot of jobs in my long life."

Marie-Louise turned to Benny. "How would you like to make *tire sur la neige*?"

"I don't know," he said hesitantly. "Will I like it?"

Their guide laughed. "I think you will!"

Marie-Louise placed some of the dark, sweet liquid into a small tray. Then she led them outside once more. There, she poured the syrup in stripes on a hard-packed snowbank.

Instantly the golden syrup turned into sugar strips.

"That is sugar-on-snow candy," she told them. "Try it!" From her pocket, she pulled out plastic forks.

Benny used his fork to pick up the maple taffy. "Yummy!" he said approvingly. "When I grow up, I'm going to be a syrupmaker."

Marie-Louise laughed again, then said, "Be sure to stop at the café. They serve a very good lunch."

"Sounds wonderful," said Grandfather. "Thank you for showing us around."

They walked down the path to the cedar log building. Inside, a fire crackled in the raised brick fireplace. Red-checked curtains hung at the windows. Hand-carved wooden spiles and buckets decorated the walls.

The waitress was all smiles when they first walked in, but then she frowned and crossed her arms over her chest.

"What's with her?" Violet whispered to Jessie. "She acts like she doesn't want us to come in."

"I don't know," Jessie said. "It's not like it's crowded or anything." An older couple occupied a table by the fireplace, but the restaurant was otherwise empty.

With a grudging wave, the waitress signaled the Aldens to sit at a cramped table in a far corner.

"Perhaps we could sit over there by the window?" Grandfather said politely. "Since there are five of us."

"Suit yourself," grumbled the waitress, whose name tag read BERTHILDE. She threw down a sheaf of menus written in French.

"She's not very friendly," Henry remarked.

"Maybe she's having a bad day," said

Violet. "How do we know what to order?"

"We'll get the special and hope for the best," said Grandfather. "I'm sure it'll be fine."

After a long wait, Berthilde brought them five plates of maple-baked beans, pancakes with maple syrup, and maple tarts.

"Boy, they sure like syrup around here," Jessie commented. But the food was delicious, and she ate heartily.

"I like it," said Benny. Any place that served nothing but sweets was okay in his book.

"It is good," Grandfather agreed. "But we need water or something to drink." He tried to catch the waitress's eye, but she avoided him. After a few minutes, he walked over to her and asked for some water.

Berthilde stomped back, carrying five glasses of water. She set the glasses on the table so hard, water sloshed out.

Jessie mopped the spilled water with her napkin. "The waitress is as nice as pie to those other customers, but she sure doesn't like us."

"She's never seen us before," said Grandfather. "Maybe she's tired of tourists who
don't talk to her. It's hard being a waitress."

When Berthilde returned to clear their
plates, Henry said, "We enjoyed visiting the
sugar bush today. We're staying just outside
of Nibelle, at Broken Moon Pond."

Berthilde dropped Henry's plate with a
clatter. "Broken Moon Pond! That's the old
Dupré camp, is it not?"

"Yes," replied Grandfather. "I used to
come here as a boy. Now the camp is for
sale."

The waitress made a dismissive sound.
"No one will buy that place. It's haunted!"

CHAPTER 4

"Do Not Go Back!"

"Haunted!" Violet cried loudly. "How?"

Berthilde lowered her voice dramatically. "Strange noises have been heard after dark. And things appear and disappear. It must be the work of a ghost!"

"There *is* a ghost!" Benny breathed. "I knew it!"

"Do not go back to Broken Moon Pond!" Berthilde warned. "Get in your car and drive home."

"The camp is not haunted," Grandfather

said reasonably. "You know ghosts aren't real, Benny. Anyway, we're staying for the sugar festival."

Outside, the children began speaking all at once.

"Suppose the camp *is* haunted," Benny said.

"We did find a boat," Violet added. "But when we tried to show it to the Anderson kids, it was gone."

In the car, Grandfather spoke firmly, "I'm sure there is a logical explanation for everything."

"That's what I think," Henry put in. "What was strange was the way that waitress acted."

"Henry's right," agreed Jessie. "She didn't want to serve us, that's for sure. And when she did, she dropped things and forgot our drinks."

"Maybe she's new at that job," suggested Grandfather as they drove into Nibelle. "I'm going to stop at the market and pick up something for dinner."

He parked in front of the real estate

agency. The children decided to wait outside.

"Look," Benny said, pointing to a blue station wagon next to them. "That's the Andersons' car."

"And here they come out of the office," said Violet. "I wonder if they bought Broken Moon Pond. Let's go talk to them!"

Patty met them with a glum face. "Hi, guys. We didn't buy the camp yet."

"Why not?" asked Jessie.

"Mr. Cartier couldn't find the phone number of one of the guys selling the camp," Aaron answered.

Jessie could tell he was disappointed. "Mr. Cartier isn't very organized," she said. "He gave us the wrong keys because his assistant is away. His files are a mess, I bet." If Jessie worked there, she'd be able to find every single piece of paper.

"I have a weird feeling about all of this," Patty said.

"What kind of weird feeling?" Violet asked.

Patty shrugged. "I'm not sure. But something isn't right. People in this town treat us like — well, like they don't want us here."

The Alden children looked at one another. Then Henry said, "It's funny, but we have the same feeling — that people don't want *us* here, either."

Jessie had been mulling over the events of the last few days. "Strange stuff has been happening ever since we got here. First, we found that notebook —"

"What notebook?" inquired Jacob.

"A field journal," Henry said. "We believe it was kept by a kid years and years ago."

"Can we see it?" Aaron asked.

"Sure," said Jessie. "When we get back to camp. Here comes Grandfather now. Let's meet by the dock later."

James Alden stopped to speak briefly with Mr. and Mrs. Anderson. Then he put a sack of groceries in the trunk and got into the car.

Shaking his head, he said, "That's too bad about the Andersons. They are anxious to buy the camp and now there's a delay with the paperwork."

"Can you help them?" Benny wanted to know.

"I'll see what I can do," said Grandfather as they drove toward Broken Moon Pond.

Back at the camp, the kids put away the groceries.

Jessie retrieved the field journal from her dresser, then made sure everyone had sweaters in case it became chilly again.

They ran outside and down to the pond. The sun was out, dappling the water with golden sparkles.

Patty, Aaron, and Jacob were waiting by the dock.

"Emma's taking a nap," Patty said. "She's a good kid, but she's too little to hang out with us. Is that the journal?"

Jessie held it out. "Be careful. It's really old."

Patty took the book and slowly turned the pages. "Wow. This kid was a good artist. Look at that owl. It looks real."

The owl picture was Benny's favorite, too. The artist had drawn the owl flying against a full moon. The bird seemed as if it were swooping off the page.

At the top, a wing feather had been sketched in detail. Beneath the feather was a single word. Benny was about to ask what the word was when Patty turned the page.

The next drawing showed a wildcat with long, thick fur and tufted ears.

"What is that?" asked Violet, trying to read upside down. "A lynx? I've never heard of it."

Henry nodded. "I have. It's related to the bobcat, only more rare. People used to hunt them for their fur. I wonder if the kid who drew this actually saw one."

"He must have," said Violet. "This drawing wasn't made from a photograph. It was done fast, as if he were watching the cat from someplace high. See the angle?"

Now that Violet pointed it out, Jessie could see the cat was sketched quickly but expertly. Still, the energy of the cat came through in only a few pencil strokes.

"Let's take a hike," suggested Jacob. "We haven't done much walking since we got here."

"We haven't, either," said Henry. "Excellent idea."

Jessie tucked the field notebook in her pocket and they walked around the pond and onto a path just beyond the camp.

"Boy, it's creepy in here," Benny remarked as they entered the woods.

"Canadian forests are pretty dense," Aaron said. "The evergreen trees make it dark in here."

Just then something rustled in a nearby shrub.

"Look!" Patty cried.

A brown animal with a white stomach, long ears, and huge feet bounded out of the brush.

"That's the biggest bunny I've ever seen!" Benny exclaimed.

Henry chuckled. "It wasn't a bunny, Benny. That was a snowshoe hare."

"Hair?" Puzzled, Benny tugged at his own bangs.

"No, a hare," Henry explained. "It's related to the rabbit, but different. The babies are born with fur and their eyes open. Baby rabbits are born without fur and their eyes shut."

"There's a picture in the journal," said Jessie, pulling the notebook from her pocket. "Here it is. You're right, Henry. That was a snowshoe hare. The artist drew it in its spring phase, it says. Brown and white. In the winter, it would be all white, to blend in with the snow. And in the summer, it's brown."

"This notebook is great," Aaron remarked. "I never knew so much about animals before."

As they walked on, they made other discoveries. Violet spotted the tiny tracks of a deer mouse on a snowy bank. They knew the tracks were made by a deer mouse because the artist had drawn them in the notebook.

"I wish we knew who this person was," Jessie said wistfully. "I feel like we know him, through his drawings."

"How come you say 'he'?" asked Patty. "It could be a 'she.'"

"I don't think so," said Jessie. "I don't know why, but I feel like the person who kept this notebook was a boy."

Violet was watching a flock of geese fly overhead, heading north. *Has there ever been a prettier sight?* she wondered. It was so peaceful in the woods, with birds and animals around.

Then she had a thought.

"I think the person was here," she said suddenly.

"Where?" Henry asked.

"Right here, in these woods," Violet answered. "I can't explain it. Like Jessie, it's just a feeling I have."

"Do you think his ghost is here?" Benny asked fearfully.

Violet patted her little brother's shoulder. "No, not his ghost. It's like the feeling we get when we're in an old house. You can tell it's been lived in by other people a long time ago. I believe the journal-keeper walked where we are years and years ago."

The kids stopped at a fork in the path.

"Which way?" asked Jacob.

"Let's go that way," said Henry, pointing right.

He didn't know why, but he had a feeling that something important was at the end of the trail.

The path wound around a steep hill. Then the dense woods opened up into a clearing.

The children pushed brambles away, staring with round eyes.

In the center of the clearing stood an immense black maple tree with wide-spreading branches.

And nestled among the sturdy branches was a wondrous sight.

CHAPTER 5

The Amazing, Fantastic Tree House!

Violet gasped. "Wow!"

"Amazing!" said Aaron, awestruck.

"Fantastic," was Jessie's reaction.

Benny summed it up. "It's an amazing, fantastic tree house!"

And it was. None of the children had ever seen a tree house like this one.

Sheltered by the welcoming branches of the maple, the tree house had been built on three levels. The main part curved around the trunk, with the tree growing out of the center of the roof. A catwalk surrounded the larger structure on all four sides.

Above the main section were two smaller additions, one above the other. They were reached by stairs. Each section had a slanted shingled roof and glass windows. A large railed platform topped off the fantastic dwelling.

"What a neat place!" Benny exclaimed, running to the bottom of the tree. "How do we get up there?"

Henry glanced around for a ladder or handholds. But nothing was nailed to the bark of the huge maple.

"I see a hole cut in the platform," he said, tipping his head back. "But where is the ladder?"

Violet noticed a wooden stick near the base of the tree. *That's funny*, she thought. The branches started way up. Why was one growing so near the roots?

Then she saw the knobby top of the branch had been carved like an owl's head.

"Look," she said, touching the owl's head.

As she did, a ladder dropped from the platform overhead. The ladder was made of thickly woven rope.

Jessie stared at her sister in astonishment. "How did you do that?"

"I don't know," Violet replied, amazing herself. "All I did was pull this carved thing."

Aaron and Henry studied the owl's-head stick.

"Pretty cool," Aaron pronounced. "This is really a lever. A line runs up the side of the tree, but it blends in with the bark so you can barely see it."

"When you pulled the stick, it tripped some mechanism on the platform," Henry added. "And that caused the ladder to fall down." He pushed the lever backward. The ladder was whisked up and hidden from sight.

"Cool," said Benny. "Let me try." He pulled the lever and the rope ladder fell down again.

"Who wants to go first?" asked Jacob.

"Not me," Patty replied, backing away. "I don't like heights."

"This ladder could be rotten," Henry stated. "I'm the heaviest, so I'll test it."

He put one foot in the lowest rung and bounced a little. The ladder held. Then he climbed up cautiously and pulled himself onto the platform.

With a thumbs-up signal, he said, "Who's next?"

Now everyone was eager to climb the ladder, even Patty. When they were all up on the platform, Jessie twisted the knob on the door.

"It's not locked," she remarked.

"Who would rob a tree house?" asked Benny. "Especially one that you can't get up into."

"Good point." Jessie pushed hard on the door. The hinges creaked with disuse. One by one, they all stepped inside.

No one spoke for a minute.

"This house," Henry pronounced, "is absolutely perfect."

"It's almost as nice as our boxcar," Benny said.

"But our boxcar didn't have homemade furniture," said Violet. "This furniture looks like it grew out of the tree."

Chairs were made of bent willow saplings. A single slab of cedar formed a table. Shelves had been fashioned from split logs.

"There are even pictures on the wall," Jessie commented. She particularly liked a little sign that said, TREE, SWEET TREE. "That's supposed to be 'Home, Sweet Home.' Somebody has a good sense of humor."

"And good building skills." Henry rapped the sturdy walls. "This place is completely protected from rain and wind."

"Who lives here?" Patty wanted to know, picking up a dusty pillow from a rocking chair.

"Nobody now," Violet guessed. She pointed to piles of leaves and acorns in the corners. "Squirrels did that. I don't think they'd make nests if people were around."

Benny couldn't believe anybody would

leave such a great place. The tree house was clearly someone's special hideaway.

But whose?

"I suppose we'd better go," Henry told them. "This place may not be on Broken Moon Pond's property. We could be trespassing."

"Can we come back?" asked Jacob. "Maybe the kid who built it will be here then."

Henry nodded. "Sure. But we ought to find out who owns it first."

"Maybe when you go back to the real estate agent's office, you can ask Mr. Cartier," Jessie suggested. "He might know."

They all walked out onto the platform. Henry and Aaron checked the mechanism that drew the ladder up and let it down. Henry tested the bolts the ladder was fastened to and the knots for any signs of fraying.

"Looks fine," he said. "I'll go down first to hold the ladder at the bottom so it won't sway. Violet, you follow me."

When it was Patty's turn, she said hastily, "I've changed my mind. I'll go last."

"No, you won't," Benny told her. "I'll be right behind you so nothing will happen."

"Violet and I will tell you exactly where to put your feet," Henry called up.

With the Aldens' encouragement, Patty was on the ground in no time.

Sighing with relief, she said, "Thanks a lot, you guys."

"Next time it'll be easier," Jessie said as she climbed down after Patty. "Now that you know you can do it."

Henry pushed the lever to make the ladder go up. Then they walked back through the woods the way they had come. This time they were more aware of the birds and the animals around them.

"You know," Benny said thoughtfully, "you think you're all alone in the woods, but you really aren't. You've always got company. Like that bug."

"Are you afraid of bugs, Benny?" asked Jacob.

"I'm not afraid of anything," Benny declared. Then he added, "Except maybe ghosts."

"You know there are no ghosts," Henry said to him. "You've never even seen one."

"I might," Benny said mysteriously. "If we stay here."

"Where?" asked Aaron.

They stopped at Broken Moon Pond. The setting sun cast long shadows over the dark water. Fish jumped, breaking the stillness.

"Here," Benny said dramatically. "The waitress at the café told us Broken Moon Pond is haunted."

"Really?" Aaron looked excited. "Now I hope we buy this place more than ever!"

Violet glanced across the pond. "Your dad and our grandfather are on the dock. Maybe they know something."

The kids ran around the shoreline and dashed onto the dock.

"Did we buy the camp?" Patty asked her father.

Mr. Anderson shook his head sadly. "Not

yet. One of the heirs is out of the country. He can't be contacted."

"Where is he?" asked Jacob.

"Nobody knows," said Mr. Anderson. "Mr. Cartier says he moves around a lot in his job. It could be weeks before he can be located."

The kids left the grown-ups talking and walked up the hill to the main house. They sat down on the porch steps.

"Weeks!" Patty said gloomily. "We'll never buy the camp now."

Henry looked thoughtful. "You know what?"

"What?" Aaron asked.

Henry picked up a pebble and rolled it in his palm. "I think somebody is trying to block the sale of Broken Moon Pond."

"Someone — or some*thing*," Benny added ominously.

CHAPTER 6

The Unwelcome Mat

"Some*thing*?" Patty echoed. "What do you mean?"

"What about the boat that was there one minute and gone the next?" Benny insisted. "The waitress said funny things happen here. She's right."

"I doubt there is a ghost," Henry said. "But we've noticed funny things besides the mysterious boat."

Aaron stared at him. "Are you guys some kind of detectives?"

"Yes," Benny answered proudly. "We've

solved lots of mysteries, all over the country."

Jessie tucked a strand of hair behind her ear. "We're not real detectives," she said modestly.

"But we have solved some mystery cases," Violet said. "Would you like us to try to solve yours?"

"Yes!" Patty said emphatically. "We need help."

"What are you going to do first?" Jacob wanted to know.

"Look for clues," said Jessie.

"We'll start when we go to Nibelle tomorrow," Henry said.

Although their cabin had a refrigerator and other modern appliances, Grandfather liked to buy fresh produce every day. Nibelle had a greengrocer, a store that sold nothing but fruits and vegetables.

When they went to the village the next day, Grandfather went into the greengrocer, while the children wandered around the square.

"There's a general store," said Violet. "Let's go inside. It probably has everything."

The shelves were stacked with canned goods, long underwear, mousetraps, lanterns, flyswatters, maple candy, shower caps, and jars of baby food.

Benny was fascinated by a tiny leather box. When he pulled off the lid, a thimble, needle, miniature scissors, and a coil of thread rolled out.

"I wonder how much this is," he said, checking the box for a price sticker.

"Ask the clerk," Jessie told him.

The clerk had been eyeing the children ever since they walked into the shop. He watched every move they made, Jessie noticed, as if he didn't trust them.

Now Benny approached the high counter. "Excuse me," he said, holding up the sewing kit. "How much is this?"

The clerk shrugged. *"Non Anglais."*

"What did he say?" Benny asked Jessie.

"He said he doesn't speak English." She was surprised. Throughout Quebec and even

in the village of Nibelle, most French-speaking people knew some English.

"Oh." Disappointed, Benny put the kit back on the shelf. He had wanted to buy it for Mrs. McGregor.

The kids left the shop. The wind had risen, blowing briskly through the square.

Jessie reached into her pocket and pulled out a single red-striped mitten.

"Uh-oh," she commented. "I must have dropped the other one inside the store."

She went back inside and found the mitten near a rack of magazines. Bending over to retrieve it, she heard a conversation in English. The store clerk was chatting with a man in a beige sweater. They were both speaking perfect English!

When she straightened up, the clerk saw her. Hastily, he muttered something to the other man in French.

Jessie wondered where she had seen the man in the beige sweater before. But she couldn't get a better look, since he stormed out of the store, never glancing in Jessie's direction.

Jessie hurried outside again.

"Guess what?" she said. "I heard the clerk speaking English to the man who just came out!"

"You mean the one who ran into me?" Henry countered. "He bumped my shoulder and didn't even say he was sorry — in French or English!"

"Why would the clerk pretend not to speak English?" Jessie wanted to know. "And I'm sure I've seen that man in the sweater somewhere!"

"I remember!" Violet said suddenly. "That was André Plessis! He was the guy in the sugar bush. The one at the gate who acted funny when he saw us."

"Nobody seems to like us in this town," Benny observed soberly.

"You're right, Benny," Violet agreed. "You know the welcome mat by our front door at home? Well, they put out the *un*-welcome mat here."

That evening, Grandfather and Henry built a fire in the stone fireplace while Jessie and Benny put supper on the table. Violet had volunteered to wash the dishes after supper so the others could read or take a hot bath.

While she waited for Jessie to call them to eat, she studied the field journal. *These drawings are so good*, she thought enviously.

One in particular caught her attention. The drawing of Broken Moon Pond appeared to be sketched from a great height.

She drew in her breath. "I bet the artist was in the tree house when he drew this!"

"What did you say?" Henry asked, coming over. Grandfather had gone outside for more wood.

"Look at this picture," Violet said. "See how tiny the pond is? I think the artist was up in the tree house."

Jessie came over, too. "But we can't see the pond from the tree house. There are too many trees in the way."

"Maybe those trees grew taller after the picture was drawn," Violet said. "We've never tried to see the pond. The journal is pretty old. The tree house may be that old, too."

"Let's ask Grandfather," said Benny.

When supper was ready, they all sat down.

Benny sampled the stew Jessie ladled into his bowl. "This is good, Grandfather. What is it?"

"Pork stew," replied Grandfather. "I found the recipe in an old cookbook. Because it's cold here most of the year, you need hearty food. But I made a salad, too."

Violet broke open a crusty roll and slathered on creamy butter. "Grandfather, when you used to come here, did you ever find a tree house in the woods past the pond?"

"A tree house?" he repeated. "I don't recall one."

"A big, fantastic tree house," Henry added. "You wouldn't forget it."

James Alden shook his head. "I never saw a big, fantastic tree house around here. But it sounds like you children have."

"Yeah!" Benny exclaimed. "We found it on the other side of the pond. It's really cool."

While they were having a dessert of blueberry sauce over pound cake, Violet showed Grandfather the field journal.

"When you stayed here, did you ever see this?" she asked. "Did you know the person who made these drawings?"

Grandfather studied the book. "This sketchbook is old," he pronounced. "But it's not old enough to be from the time when I was a boy. These drawings are excellent." He looked up. "You children have been busy making discoveries. A fantastic tree house . . . this journal . . ."

As they cleared the table, Violet said, "I have to know for sure. Let's go to the tree house now and check out that drawing."

"We're going out for a walk," Henry told Grandfather, taking his jacket from the hook by the front door.

"Don't be long," Grandfather cautioned. "It'll be dark soon."

The chilly air hurried the children down

the path past the pond and into the woods. The lingering light over the trees was a hard, bright blue.

The clearing was quiet and still. At the tree house, Benny pulled the owl's head lever and the rope ladder dropped down.

They quickly climbed up to the catwalk.

"Up here," Henry said, scaling the small handholds set into the trunk to the balcony above the second level.

"I don't think I've ever been this high up in a tree," said Jessie. Now she knew how Patty felt.

Violet took the field journal from her pocket and opened it to the drawing of Broken Moon Pond. Then she gazed out over the treetops. Just beyond was a shimmering speck — the pond.

"I see it!" she cried. "I was right!"

"Good work," Henry praised. "Now we know two things. One, the notebook and this tree house were made after Grandfather was here. But both are still old. And two, it's possible the same person who used this tree house was the artist."

"How does that help us solve the mystery of the ghost boat?" asked Benny.

"Or the problem the Andersons are having buying the camp?" said Jessie.

"These clues don't help us yet," said Henry. "We'd better head back before Grandfather starts to worry."

At the cabin, the children went to their rooms to get ready for bed.

Benny pulled up the covers, yawning hugely. Grandfather's pork stew had made him extra sleepy. He drifted off to sleep as soon as Henry switched off the light.

Screech! Scree-eech!

Benny sat up with a start. *What was that?* he wondered.

CHAPTER 7

The Ghost Boat Returns

"Henry!" Benny whispered. "Do you hear that?"

Henry sat up, too, and listened.

Scree-ee-ee! Scree!

"What *is* that?" he asked Benny.

"I don't know."

Together they rushed to the window. The moon was riding high in a cloudless sky. Nearly full, it looked like a bite had been chewed out on one side.

"Down there!" Benny said, pointing to the pond below.

Henry froze. "Go get Violet and Jessie, please. They should see this."

Within seconds, Benny was back with his sisters. "Is it still there?" he asked Henry.

Henry nodded, then made room for Jessie and Violet at the window.

Jessie gasped. "It's the boat—!"

"With nobody rowing it," Violet finished.

"And we heard a weird sound," Benny said.

"So did we!" exclaimed Jessie.

"I think that noise is being made by a person," Henry stated.

"What about the boat?" asked Benny. "I don't see a person."

"Benny," said Henry. "That boat is not being rowed by a ghost."

"But it's empty and it's moving across the water!" His eyes were not fooling him.

"I'm sure there's an explanation," Henry said.

But he didn't know what it could be. This was a baffling mystery. How was the boat moving across the pond? And what was that terrible sound he and Benny had heard?

"We need to find that boat," said Violet. "Then maybe we'll find the ghost." She shivered. She didn't *really* want to find the ghost of Broken Moon Pond.

After a breakfast of omelettes, maple-drenched French toast, and link sausages, the Aldens ran down the hill to the pond. The Anderson kids were waiting on the bank.

"You guys are always up early," Jessie commented.

"Thanks to Emma," said Patty with a grin.

"Yeah," added Aaron. "Try sleeping with a two-year-old around. Did you find out anything about our case?"

Jessie told them about the empty boat they had seen moving across the water and the strange sounds they had all heard.

"A ghost boat!" said Jacob. "Maybe our ghost likes to fish."

"The boat was here," Jessie concluded. "This is near where we found the boat the first time."

"A ghost wouldn't be strong enough to shove a boat away from the shore," Violet added. "But a *person* could."

"Like who?" asked Patty.

Henry straightened up. "Like somebody who wants people to believe Broken Moon Pond is haunted."

"Why would they do that?" Jacob wanted to know.

Jessie thought she knew the answer. "To scare off anybody who wants to buy the camp."

"It still doesn't make sense," said Patty, frowning. "The owners *want* to sell this place."

"How many owners are there?" asked Violet.

"I think four," replied Aaron. "Counting the guy they can't find."

"Maybe not all of the owners really want to sell Broken Moon Pond," said Violet.

Henry looked at his sister with admiration. "I think you're on to something, Violet. Now if we can just figure out which one may want to block the sale."

"There's Grandfather," said Jessie, looking up at their driveway. "He's signaling for us to come. We're going into Nibelle again. Maybe we'll find out more."

Yellow banners decorated with red maple leaves swayed over Main Street. All the store windows wore signs announcing the maple sugar festival, now only two days away.

In the square, the kids stopped to read a poster.

" 'Pancake flipping contest, hayrides, a pancake breakfast, and much more,' " read Jessie. "Sounds like fun. We're going, aren't we, Grandfather?"

"Wouldn't miss it for the world," said James Alden. "I'll be just a few minutes in the courthouse."

The children wandered to the other side of the street. One store displayed a pyramid of maple syrup tins to advertise the festival.

Benny licked his lips. "A whole day eating pancakes." He could hardly wait until Saturday.

Violet was looking at some stationery in the window next door. "These notebooks are a lot like the one Jessie found. Wouldn't it be neat if we started nature journals?"

"But we can't draw as well as you can, Violet," Jessie said.

"Artists always say talent doesn't matter," Violet assured her. "Anyway, we'll be doing just as much writing."

"The important thing is to record our observations about nature," said Henry. "Let's go inside. I have enough money for all of us."

They each purchased an unlined spiral notebook and a box of pencils. Then they sat on benches by the fountain. The sun felt as warm as melted butter. The trees around the square were barely beginning to bud.

"How do we start?" Benny asked Violet. "I'm not a good artist or writer."

Violet opened his notebook to the first blank page. "You draw just fine, Benny Alden. We'll help you with the writing part.

Look at that tree. What's on the end of the branches?"

Benny squinted to see better. "Little tiny leaves."

"That's an observation of nature," Henry told him. "Now try drawing a picture of the tree with those little leaves."

Soon they were all drawing and writing about the trees and birds around them.

A shadow fell over Jessie's notebook. Someone was standing behind her. She jumped, nearly dropping her pencil.

"I'm sorry," said a man's voice. "I didn't mean to startle you."

The man stood behind the bench. He wore an old sweatshirt, faded jeans with holes in the knees, and wire-framed glasses held together with tape. His shaggy gray beard needed trimming.

Benny twisted to stare at him. "Are you a hobo?" he asked.

"Benny!" Jessie smiled apologetically at the stranger. "Please excuse our little brother. We once lived in a boxcar and

we've heard stories about how people used to ride on trains and go from place to place."

The man laughed. "Well, I go from place to place, though not by boxcar. Sounds like you children have had an exciting life."

"Now we live with our grandfather," Benny told him. "And we solve mysteries."

"Really? Are you on a case at the moment?" asked the man.

"Kind of," said Jessie. "But we're taking a break now and putting entries into our nature journals."

The stranger nodded approvingly. "You have made a fine start. Remember to really *see* what you're looking at. That is the key to understanding nature. To train your eyes."

"That's what artists say," Violet agreed. "That looking and seeing aren't the same thing. Are you an art teacher?"

But when she turned around, the man had vanished.

"Where did he go?" she asked.

The square was crowded with noonday

shoppers and people going to lunch. The bearded stranger had disappeared as if by magic.

"Weird," said Henry. "This whole village is just plain weird!"

That afternoon, the Alden children met the Andersons down by the pond.

"Grandfather tried to find the property deed," said Jessie. "But they told him it's been misplaced!"

Patty shook her head. "I think our folks might be changing their minds about buying the camp."

"I hope not," said Aaron. "I really like it here."

"Let's go back to the tree house," Benny suggested.

"We didn't find out if the tree house is on this property," Henry reminded them.

"But we may find another clue," said Violet. "I still think the old journal and the tree house are tied to this mystery somehow."

"I'll bring the journal along," said Jessie.

At the tree house, Henry had trouble with the owl's-head lever that released the rope ladder.

"It seems jammed," he said, pushing on it. At last, he pushed hard enough and the ladder fell down.

"Maybe the cold weather we had last night made the lever stick," said Aaron.

When they were assembled on the catwalk above, Jessie pushed open the front door and went inside.

Instantly she saw something was different.

"Uh-oh." She dropped the journal on the floor with a thud. "Somebody is living here!"

CHAPTER 8

The Missing Page

"Someone's been here?" asked Aaron, his voice shaking. "How do you know?"

Jessie walked over to the pantry shelf. "These cans of food weren't here the other day. And the shelf is dusty. The cans are perfectly clean."

Violet nodded. "Someone brought food."

"He also left his coat." Benny pointed out a man's denim jacket hanging on a peg.

"We must be on private property," said Henry. "We'd better leave."

The children filed out of the tree house. Henry closed the door behind him.

They were halfway back to the pond when Jessie clapped her hand to her mouth.

"The journal! I dropped it in the tree house!"

"Should we go back and get it?" Jacob wondered.

"It belongs to the cabin," said Jessie. "We have to."

They hurried back to the clearing and climbed the ladder once more. Henry came up last.

"I thought you shut the door," Violet said to him.

"I did." He tested the knob. The door pushed open easily. "Maybe the wind blew it open."

But it's not windy today, he thought.

"Here it is," Jessie said, quickly fetching the notebook off the table. "Let's get out of here. This place is giving me the creeps."

It wasn't until after lunch that Jessie remembered something else. She had

dropped the journal on the *floor*. How did
it get on the table? Leafing through the
journal, she made a startling discovery.

"There's a page missing," she declared.

The others gathered around her chair.

"See?" Jessie pointed to a ragged strip of
paper near the back. "Somebody ripped out
that page."

"Why would he tear out one page?"
asked Violet.

"The question is," said Jessie, "*where* was
he?"

Henry was wondering about that, too.
"The person must have been in the tree
house between the time we left and the
time we went back for the notebook. That's
when he ripped out the page."

"Where could he have been?" Violet
asked.

"Maybe in the high part of the tree
house," suggested Benny.

The children exchanged uneasy glances.
Someone must have been watching them
while they entered the tree house the first
time.

"Are you sure this page wasn't missing before?" Violet asked Jessie.

"Positive," Jessie said firmly. "I would remember the torn pieces. I wish I knew what was on that page." She tapped the leather cover as if trying to jog her memory.

"I know what was on it," Benny stated.

"What?" asked Jessie.

"A picture of an owl," he replied. "It had a word beside it, but I couldn't read it."

Violet nodded. "I remember that picture, too. It was flying across the moon. I don't remember the word, though."

Jessie flipped through the journal. "No owl picture. That must be the missing page. Now we have to figure out why someone stole that page."

"And who did it," Henry said solemnly. "We saw a man's jacket in the tree house. But that doesn't mean our mystery person is a man."

"Everything is so confusing," said Jessie. "First there's the disappearing boat. Then there are those unfriendly people in the village."

"Don't forget the Andersons' problem," Violet added. "And now the stranger in the tree house."

"There's only one thing we can do," Benny said.

"What?" the others chorused.

"Go outside and play!" was his answer.

Henry patted his brother on the back. "Excellent idea!"

Outside, the Aldens sorted the jumble of sports equipment on the big porch.

"Snowshoes, ice skates, cross-country skis, sleds," said Grandfather. "We used all of these things when I came here as a boy."

Benny strapped on the snowshoes. He stood up and stumbled.

"How do people ever walk in these?" he asked.

Grandfather laughed. "You're supposed to wear them in the snow. I think you might get your chance to try out this equipment. Maybe tomorrow."

"Snow?" said Jessie.

"It isn't unusual to have a big snow in the spring in Canada," said Grandfather. "It could be a problem, though, with the maple syrup production."

"They won't cancel the party, will they?" Benny asked.

"They'll have the festival no matter what," James Alden reassured them. "But if there's a storm, they may not be able to finish the sugar run."

"We'd better play outdoors while we can," said Henry.

"And I should drive to town for extra groceries," Grandfather said. "Just in case."

"We'll stay here," Jessie said. "I see the Anderson kids at the pond, and Mr. and Mrs. Anderson are here."

After Grandfather drove off, the Aldens walked down to the pond. Aaron and Jacob had made a model sailboat from a kit. They were launching it from the shore, while Patty gave them orders.

A small breeze lifted the sail and scooted it sideways across the water. The boat disappeared in the reeds.

"I told you not to let it go there," Patty said to her brothers.

"I'll get it," Benny volunteered. He was closest to that side of the pond.

Benny stepped carefully through the muck at the edge of the waterline. The boat was bobbing just out of reach. He found a stick and prodded it loose. The boat caught the breeze again and sailed across the ruffled pond.

As he turned to leave, he saw something in the thick reeds. Another boat, much bigger than the toy boat.

"Come see what I found!" he cried.

In a flash, the others joined him.

Jessie drew in a breath. "It's the boat Violet and I saw the first night we were here."

"Henry and I saw it, too," Benny put in. "It's the ghost boat!"

"That old thing?" questioned Aaron. "I bet it leaks."

Violet said, "It says *Orville*. That's the same boat, all right."

"*Orville?*" repeated Benny. He looked at the painted letters. "I think that's the word printed on the owl page in the nature journal."

"Maybe this boat and the owl page are connected," Henry said.

Jessie was poking around the side of the boat. "Look at this."

She pointed to an eye hook screwed into the hull. About a foot of frayed green nylon rope was looped around the hook.

"That's weird," said Jacob. "Why would anybody tie up their boat with the hook way down there?"

"It's not used to tie the boat," Henry said, tugging on the frayed rope. "I bet our 'ghost' stands on the dock and pulls the boat across the pond. With the rope at the bottom, you wouldn't see it."

"So it looks like an empty boat going across the water by itself," said Violet. "Now all we have to do is find the 'ghost.' "

"We're leaving after the sugar festival," Henry said. "That gives us two days to solve all these mysteries."

After supper, Grandfather made a fire and sat down with a book.

The children washed and dried the

dishes. While they worked, they discussed the mystery.

"Most of the strange things around here have happened at night," Violet observed.

"Violet's right," agreed Jessie. "Let's go outside. Maybe the 'ghost' will appear again and we can catch him. Or her."

Wiping crumbs off the table, Henry said, "Grandfather, may we go out for a few minutes? We'd like some air."

"Dress warmly," said James Alden. "And don't go far."

The children slipped into jackets and mittens and scarves. Outside, they hopped off the porch and ran partway down the hill to the pond.

"This is far enough," Henry told the others. "We're away from the lights of the cabin, so we won't be seen."

They waited, watching for any movement on the still pond.

Overhead, the moon was still mostly full, though tattered clouds drifted across it.

Violet thought the moon looked bigger here than back home, possibly because they

were away from the lights in town. She shivered, wondering if the "ghost" would show up. What would they do if it did?

Just then she heard a horrible sound.

Scree-eech! Scree!

"What is it?" she whispered. "Is it the ghost?"

Henry shook his head. "There is no ghost. The boat we found proves that human hands have been pulling it across the pond." But *what* was making that sound?

Screee-eeech!

Suddenly the scudding clouds parted. Henry saw a dark winged shape gliding against the pale surface of the moon.

He knew what was making the horrible sound.

CHAPTER 9

Snowstorm!

"What is *that*?" Benny exclaimed. He moved closer to his big brother.

"I think I know," said Henry. "Let's go back inside."

In the cabin, Henry went to the bookshelves and pulled down a well-worn guidebook.

"Aha! I thought so." He turned the book so the others could see. "That sound we heard is the call of a screech owl."

"Is that what we've been hearing all along?" asked Jessie.

"Maybe." Henry paused. "I still think a person was making that noise the other night. It didn't sound exactly the same."

Violet studied the picture. "I bet this is the same owl as the one in the nature journal."

Benny thought of something. "We keep seeing owls around here."

"That's right," Jessie said. "The owl's-head stick at the tree house . . . the picture in the journal . . . and now a real one."

"Definitely a pattern," Henry murmured, putting the guidebook back in the bookcase.

Yet, the pieces did not add up.

"Snow!" Benny leaped from bed the next morning. "Henry, it's snowing!"

Henry went to the window. "Looks pretty deep. It must have started snowing during the night."

Downstairs, the children quickly ate Grandfather's egg-and-sausage casserole with cranberry muffins. For once, Benny didn't pile his plate with a second helping.

"What's your hurry?" James Alden asked him with a wink.

"The snow!" Benny cried. "We want to go out and play!"

"I'm afraid you can't do that yet," said Grandfather.

"Why not?" said Violet. She was eager to sled down the big hill.

"The sugar bush workers will have to finish the run today," Grandfather said, carrying the casserole dish to the sink. "Do you want to help them?"

"Make syrup?" This was a dream come true for Benny. Even snow could wait. "You bet!"

After cleaning up the dishes, the Aldens dressed in jeans and sweaters, then climbed into the rental car.

Grandfather drove slowly. The woods were a frosty wonderland.

The guardhouse was abandoned at the sugar camp. Grandfather parked in the snow-covered lot near the sugar hut.

Trucks prowled up and down the snowy lanes between the maple trees. Some were loaded with last night's sap, while others carried empty gathering tanks into the woods to collect more sap.

Benny inhaled as he got out of the car. The sweet aroma of maple sugar filled the air.

"This smells better than any perfume," he commented as they headed for the *cabane*.

"No wonder people eat pancakes all day long," Violet said with a giggle. "The syrup smell makes them hungry!"

Inside the sugar hut, workers scurried back and forth, checking thermometers, pouring syrup into tins, turning valves connected to vats of simmering sap.

Marie-Louise, their guide from their first visit, waved when she saw the Aldens. Today she wore her long red hair tied back. An apron covered her jeans and blue shirt.

"We've come to help," Grandfather told her. "I've had some experience in making

sugar and my grandchildren are good workers. I hope you can use us."

"How kind of you!" she said. "With this
snow, we need every pair of hands."

Grandfather was assigned to working with
another man on an evaporator.

Benny and Henry unloaded raw sap from
the gathering tanks as the trucks pulled in.
The sap was funneled through a tube that
led directly into the hut and into another
gathering tank.

Jessie and Violet were assigned to help
Marie-Louise grade syrup.

"I will do the testing," she told the girls.
"You can paste labels on the bottles. The
law requires us to mark the grade and color
class of syrup on every container."

She poured syrup from a flat pan into
bottles.

"What a pretty color," Violet remarked.
"Like my amber crayon, only it's see-
through."

"*Oui*," Marie-Louise agreed, selecting a
strip of preprinted labels that read CANADA

#1, EXTRA LIGHT. "This grade and color is the most desirable. We were fortunate to make several high-quality batches this year."

She screwed on metal caps, then set each bottle on its side on a shelf. The containers were spaced far apart.

"Shouldn't we turn them upright?" Jessie asked. "And put them closer together?"

Marie-Louise shook her head. "The syrup is always poured hot into the containers. Placing each bottle on its side sterilizes the cap and neck. If the bottles are placed close together as they cool, the syrup has what we call 'stack burn,' an unpleasant aftertaste."

Violet wiped her forehead. It was quite warm in the sugar hut. "I never knew there was so much to learn about making syrup."

"We will have demonstrations at the festival tomorrow," said Marie-Louise. "But you are learning the best way—by doing!"

While the girls pasted on labels, Marie-Louise left to get another pan of finished syrup.

Suddenly one of the workers, who was

passing the small window, looked out. His mouth formed a shocked O.

"Zut alors!" he cried. *"L'homme qui habite dans la maison en arbre!"*

Everyone except the Aldens stopped working and raced to the window. They all crowded around, pointing and remarking in rapid French.

Henry wanted to see what all the fuss was about, too, but then he noticed an unattended evaporator.

"Benny, nobody is watching that batch of syrup," he said. "Grandfather is busy at his own evaporator. We'd better go over there."

The evaporator consisted of a metal pan with a propane-fueled stove beneath.

Henry knew the pans had to be watched carefully. "The temperature can't get too high or the whole batch will be ruined."

Benny looked at the thermometer. "It says 215. How high is it supposed to go?"

"No higher than 218 degrees," Henry said. The syrup was nearly ready. All the workers were still clustered at the window, talking to one another excitedly.

The mercury on the thermometer rose steadily: 216 . . . 217. Hot bubbles popped in the amber liquid. Another few seconds and the batch would be ruined!

How can we get the workers' attention? Henry wondered.

Then Benny exclaimed, *"Zut alors!"*

Everyone at the window turned to stare at him.

"The syrup's ready!" he said.

At once, three workers lurched across the room and removed the covered pan from the stove.

Marie-Louise came over with Jessie and Violet.

"I didn't know you could speak French," she said, teasing Benny.

"I just said what that man said," Benny explained with a shrug. "But I don't know what it means!"

The Aldens helped until noon. By then it was clear the workers would finish the run before the festival.

"See you tomorrow," Marie-Louise said

before they left. "Admission will be free. That is the least we can do, since you helped us so much. We are very grateful."

It had stopped snowing. As Grandfather drove through the gate, the children saw a familiar figure in the guardhouse.

André Plessis.

When he saw the Aldens, he glanced away guiltily. Violet noticed something hanging out of his pocket. Since she was sitting up front with Grandfather, she decided to wait until they were at the cabin before mentioning it to the others.

"I wonder what that man said that made everyone run to look out the window," said Henry as they drove out.

Jessie was already thumbing through her French-English dictionary. "I remember some of it. He said, 'Man who lives in the house of the tree.' "

"*What?*" asked Benny.

"I think he was talking about a man who lives in a tree house," Jessie replied.

Grandfather shook his head. "Whoever the man is, he certainly got the workers excited."

Jessie exchanged a look with Henry. Grandfather was right. The man who lived in the tree house obviously knew something. They needed to find him and get some answers.

Maybe he was the key to the strange happenings at Broken Moon Pond.

The Anderson kids were waiting for the Aldens on the porch of the main cabin.

"Where have you been?" asked Patty.

Violet explained about their morning. Then she added, "André Plessis had a piece of green nylon rope hanging out of his pocket. I saw it. It was just like the one tied to the *Orville* boat!"

"I bet anything that André is our 'ghost,' " Henry concluded.

"That's probably why he looked so guilty today," said Jessie. "He knows he isn't fooling us."

"We've found something, too!" said

Aaron. "But we have to wear snowshoes."

The children strapped on the snowshoes stacked on the porch. Trying to walk in the fluffy snow made them laugh until they got the hang of it.

"Here!" said Patty. "Look at these!"

Down by the pond, fresh footprints marked the snow. The tracks led into the woods, toward the tree house.

"I bet these prints take us right to the tree house!" said Jessie. "They must belong to the man who lives there."

They set off into the trees. When they reached the clearing, Violet, who was in front, gave a cry.

At the base of the huge maple tree lay a crumpled figure.

CHAPTER 10

Benny's Guess

Violet said, "That's the man we saw in the square the other day!"

Henry was the first to reach him. The bearded man was lying on his side with one leg twisted beneath him. Henry checked the man's breathing, then peered into his eyes.

"He's conscious," Henry concluded. Carefully, he straightened the man's bent leg and felt his ankle.

When the man moaned, Jessie asked, "Is it broken?"

"Sprained, I think."

The boys helped the man sit up.

"Do I feel foolish," the man said, his teeth showing in a rueful grin through his beard. "I guess I'm not as young as I think!"

"Can you stand?" Henry asked him.

The big man struggled to his feet, then winced with pain. "Not very well."

"He needs to get inside," said Jessie. "His clothes are wet."

"Violet, find some strong branches," Henry said. He took off his scarf and wound it around the man's ankle.

Violet returned with several sturdy branches. Henry chose two that were long enough to fit under the injured man's arms.

With Henry and Aaron on either side of the man, the children snowshoed through the woods to Broken Moon Pond. When they led him up to the main cabin, the man nodded.

"I know my way, thank you," he said.

He limped inside, with the Aldens and Andersons trailing, and sank into the nearest chair.

Grandfather turned from the stove. "I see we have a guest. I'm James Alden. And you are?"

"Orville," Benny blurted.

Everyone stared at him.

"Orville?" repeated Jessie. "Where on earth did you get that name?" She knew the stranger hadn't spoken a word during their trek through the woods.

The man laughed. "The lad is right. My name *is* Orville!"

"How did you know that?" Henry asked Benny.

Benny shrugged. "I just guessed. That was the name on the boat we found. I bet it's the name on the owl page in the nature journal. And . . . he *looks* like an Orville."

Grandfather smiled. "You made what is known as an educated guess. I can see you are injured, Orville. Benny, would you bring that stool over?"

Henry helped the man take off his wet jacket and boots. Violet draped one of the plaid wool blankets over his shoulders while Jessie fixed a pot of tea.

With his foot propped up, Orville sighed with relief. "Much better, thank you. I feel foolish falling out of my own tree house. But I suppose I shouldn't have tried to climb that slippery ladder at my age."

"You built the tree house!" Jessie exclaimed.

"I did indeed," Orville replied. "My parents owned this camp. I became interested in nature when I was about Benny's age."

"You kept a notebook," said Patty. "We've seen it."

Orville sipped his tea. "That notebook was the start of my career. I'm a naturalist — a special kind of scientist. I still watch birds and animals, only now I take photographs."

Grandfather snapped his fingers. "Now I remember where I've seen your name! You're Orville Dupré—I've seen your work in many nature magazines."

Orville nodded. "It's an interesting life and I'm suited to it. I was a loner as a child.

I preferred drifting on the pond in my boat or drawing in my notebook. I built the tree house to better observe wildlife."

"That's some tree house!" Henry said admiringly. "A person could live in it."

"I did," Orville said with a chuckle. "Not all the time, because I soon grew weary of eating canned beans."

Benny had a thought. "You like owls, don't you? That's why you carved an owl on the stick that makes the ladder come down."

"I am fond of screech owls. Now perhaps you can answer a question for me. Where did you find my field notebook?" asked Orville.

"It was stuck in the dresser in the bedroom Violet and I are using," replied Jessie. "We take it with us on our walks in the woods. Yesterday I left the notebook behind in the tree house. When we found it, somebody had torn a page out."

"I did it," Orville admitted. "I was looking through my journal when I accidentally ripped that page. I wondered how my notebook suddenly appeared in the tree house. Then when I came back today, it was gone again. I thought maybe I had dropped it off the catwalk. I was going out to look for it when I fell off the ladder."

"I used to come here as a boy myself," said Grandfather. "I don't remember you, though."

Orville chuckled again. "There were a lot of Dupré children. My cousins and I were forever running in and out of the cabins, hiking in the woods, swimming in the pond. I miss the camp. This is my first time back in years."

"Why don't you live here?" Benny asked. If he owned that neat tree house, he'd stay in it forever.

"My work takes me all over the world," replied Orville. "I'm not in one spot for very long."

Grandfather brought a pot of potato soup to the table. As he served everyone, he said, "I suppose that's why you are selling Broken Moon Camp."

Orville looked downcast. "I wish my cousins and I could keep the place. But they don't come here anymore, and I need the money."

"My parents would like to buy the camp," Aaron told him. "We love it here."

"Why, that's wonderful!" Orville said. "I would be delighted to see Broken Moon Pond owned by caring people."

"The Andersons have been discouraged from buying the camp," Henry stated.

Orville looked surprised. "Discouraged? How?"

"The ghost boat, for one thing," Jessie answered.

"Ghost boat?" Orville frowned in confusion.

Violet hastily explained. "It's not really a ghost. At night, somebody pulled your old boat across the pond to make it look like a ghost was rowing it."

"Then the boat disappeared," said Jessie. "After we found it."

"Very peculiar," said Orville.

"And there was that scary noise," Benny added. He imitated the sound.

"The screech owl," said Orville. "They call out at night around here."

"We saw one last night," Henry said. "But other times, I think a person was making the noise to scare us."

Grandfather frowned. "I don't understand. The Andersons are buying the camp. Why would someone try to scare *us*?"

"I think I have that figured out," said Jessie. She spoke to Orville. "The caretaker left before we got here. He didn't meet the Andersons, either. But he knew a family with four children was making an offer on the camp. The person who wanted to scare off the buyer didn't know which family it was."

"So they tried to scare us, too?" asked Benny. "Just to be on the safe side?"

Orville put down his soup spoon. "None of this makes sense. My cousins and I wish to sell. We don't want to frighten anyone off!"

"We thought maybe one of the sellers

was trying to block the sale for some reason," said Henry.

Orville shook his head. "It isn't anyone in my family. I have no idea who might be blocking the sale of Broken Moon Pond."

Jessie was busy thinking. The clues had always pointed to different people — the clerk in the store who pretended not to speak English, the waitress at the café who gave them bad service, André Plessis. . . . Now the pieces clicked into place.

"I know who is behind all this," she announced.

Everyone turned toward her.

"Who?" asked Grandfather.

"Well, I thought about the strange things that have happened, like the man in the store who spoke English, but not to us," she began. "It seemed like everybody was a suspect. But why would the village shopkeeper try to keep the Andersons from buying Broken Moon Pond?"

Violet grabbed Jessie's arm in her excitement. "It isn't any one person, is it?"

"No, it's *all* of them!" Jessie said triumphantly.

"Wow!" said Henry, impressed. "How did you come up with this?"

Jessie grinned. "I made a good guess!"

At that moment, someone knocked at the door. Grandfather got up to answer it.

André Plessis stood in the doorway. He saw Orville inside and exclaimed, "It is you! My old friend! You have come back!"

"Please come in," said Grandfather. "And join us."

"Thank you," André said. "But I have eaten." He sat down at the table.

"André and I grew up together," Orville said to the Aldens. "I taught him how to imitate the call of the screech owl."

"That was you!" Henry accused. "You were outside our cabin making that sound!"

André ducked his head.

"And you pulled the boat at night," added Benny. "I bet you made the boat disappear, too."

"Yes," André admitted. "I did those things. I am not proud of it."

"But why?" asked Orville. "Why would you bother the Aldens with tricks?"

"I thought they were buying the camp," André replied. "We heard in town a family with four children wanted to buy Broken Moon Pond. This camp has always been in your family. It should not be sold."

"So you tried to discourage the buyers," said Orville. "Only you 'scared' the wrong family!"

"I thought the villagers were protecting 'tree house man,'" Jessie said to Orville. "When they saw you outside the sugar hut, they were startled. They acted like *they* had seen a ghost."

"It has been many years since I was here last," said Orville. "The people of Nibelle are proud of my work as a naturalist."

"They probably feel Broken Moon Pond is rightfully yours," Grandfather agreed.

"Who else was in on this scheme?" Orville asked André.

"Claude, at the general store," André answered. "He pretended not to speak English when the children were in his shop. Also Berthilde at the café. She gave the Aldens bad service and then told them the camp was haunted."

"You should be ashamed!" Orville said. "I will straighten this out with the Anderson family. But I can't walk on this ankle yet. Could they come here?"

The Anderson children fetched their parents. Orville and André explained the situation and apologized on behalf of Nibelle.

"If the villagers are this loyal, they must be great people," said Mr. Anderson. "We still want to buy the camp."

"Wonderful," said Orville. "I ask only one thing — that I be allowed to visit my tree house whenever I can."

"We wouldn't even have known about the tree house if the Alden children hadn't found it," said Mrs. Anderson.

"My grandchildren have a way of finding things," said Grandfather affectionately. "Especially mysteries!"

*　*　*

The sun shone brightly the next morning, melting the snow. It would be a great day for the sugar festival.

Orville had stayed with the Aldens the night before. His ankle was better and he rode with them to Nibelle.

The narrow streets were jammed with booths and people. Balloons bobbled from every lamppost.

"I'm entering the log-sawing contest!" Henry said.

"I'll enter the pancake-flipping contest," said Grandfather. "They are using snow shovels to flip the pancakes! That ought to be a challenge!"

Benny found his own contest.

A tower of pancakes was displayed on a table, next to a huge jug of syrup. Benny wanted to win that syrup for Mrs. McGregor.

"What do I do?" he asked the lady tending the booth.

"Tell me how many pancakes are in the stack," she replied. "Just give me your best guess."

Benny looked hard at the stack. Then he guessed right!

"That really *was* your best guess!" Henry said to Benny as he helped him lift the prize jug.

"What's your secret?" Jessie asked.

Benny shrugged. "I guess best when I'm hungry!"

The Aldens laughed.

A Puzzling Pond

It's late spring and the Alden family is heading north. This time, Henry, Jessie, Violet, and Benny are visiting Broken Moon Pond, a favorite childhood vacation site for Grandfather Alden located in Quebec, Canada.

Though the scenic area looks peaceful, the not-so-friendly people and strange occurrences make for a mysterious vacation. Is there really a ghost at Broken Moon Pond? Or is there another explanation for these haunting happenings? The Aldens are determined to find the answers!

Turn the page to begin testing your own puzzle-solving skills. You can check your answers at the back of the book. Good luck!

Key Caper

When the Alden family arrives at their cabin, they find that the real estate agent, Mr. Cartier, has given them the wrong key. There are ten keys shown below, but only one of them fits the lock on the cabin door. Can you tell which key is the correct one? It's the only one that is different from the others.

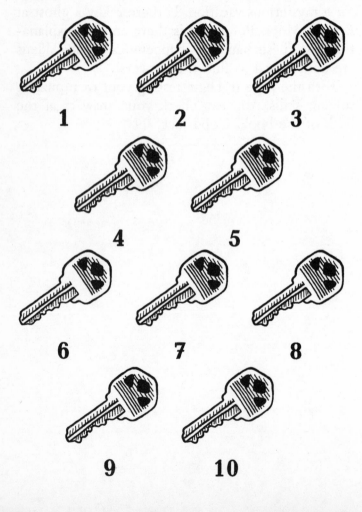

Mmm-mmm, Good!

The Aldens have arrived in Quebec at the perfect time of year — sugaring season! The people of the small village near Broken Moon Pond make maple syrup each year from the sap of the maple trees. What's the perfect food to eat with maple syrup? Pancakes, of course! See how many three-, four-, and five-letter words you can make from the word PANCAKES. Ten is good, twenty is great, and twenty-five is pancake perfection!

P A N C A K E S

_____	_____
_____	_____
_____	_____
_____	_____
_____	_____
_____	_____
_____	_____
_____	_____
_____	_____

Canadian Crossword

Henry, Jessie, Violet, and Benny all agree that Broken Moon Pond is in a beautiful part of Canada. But it's just one of many spectacular sites that can be found in this northern country. Use the map below to help you answer the clues about places in Canada. Then fill in the puzzle.

Across

4. Borders on eastern Alberta
5. Borders on eastern British Columbia
6. British _____, on the west coast

Down

1. Borders on eastern Ontario
2. Borders on western Ontario
3. Found between Manitoba and Quebec

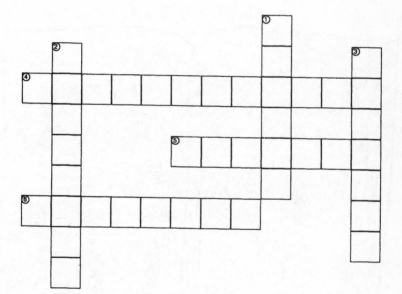

Field Journal Fun

When Jessie finds an old notebook filled with wonderful nature drawings, she wonders whose it is. Maybe the journal is a clue to the mysterious happenings at the pond! Take a look at the forest scene below. Can you find the animals that the owner of the journal drew so many years ago? Look for a **deer**, **grasshopper**, **owl**, **lynx**, and **snowshoe hare**.

Where's Orville?

On their first night at the pond, Jessie and Violet see an old rowboat glide across the water in the moonlight — but the boat is empty! The next morning, the Aldens find the boat near the dock and notice the name *Orville* painted on its side. Can you find ORVILLE hidden in the word search below? It appears only once, and might be across, down, diagonal, or backward.

```
O  R  V  L  L  E  O  R  V  I  L  E
R  O  L  V  E  R  I  L  O  R  V  I
V  I  R  O  R  L  E  I  L  L  E  R
I  L  O  V  E  I  L  L  O  R  V  E
L  O  R  L  I  E  L  I  V  R  O  V
L  E  V  E  O  L  I  V  E  I  L  I
O  R  I  V  L  E  L  O  R  V  I  L
R  O  R  V  I  L  I  E  L  L  O  R
```

A Tasty Test

During their stay at Broken Moon, the Alden kids learn how maple syrup is made. Do you remember all of the steps in the process? Answer these questions to find out!

1. Where is the sap processed into maple syrup?
   a. Inside the tree   c. At the pond
   b. In a sugar hut

2. What does Marie-Louise use to collect the sap from the trees?
   a. A tube   c. A bucket
   b. A vacuum

3. What are the best trees for collecting sap?
   a. Maple trees   c. Palm trees
   b. Fir trees

4. What machine is used to boil away water and turn the sap into syrup?
   a. A radiator   c. An accelerator
   b. An evaporator

5. Once the sap is inside the machine, how long does it take for the sap to change into syrup?
   a. A few hours   c. A few weeks
   b. A few days

6. When the temperature reaches _____ degrees, the syrup is ready.
   a. 182   c. 218
   b. 281

An A-maze-ing Tree House

The Aldens are walking through the woods near their cabin. Henry has a feeling that something important lies deep in the forest. Can you help them all find their way to the mysterious tree house?

A Perfect Hideaway

In a clearing in the woods, the Aldens come upon the most amazing tree house they've ever seen. Built in the branches of a giant black maple tree, the tree house has three separate levels! Color the picture on the opposite page any way you like. Try to remember all that you see. Then turn the page to test your memory.

Do You Remember?

Test your memory by answering the following questions.

1. How many birds are on the roof of the third level of the tree house? _____
2. True or False: There is a deer on the left side of the clearing. _____
3. How many windows are there in total? _____
4. Which of the following is the same as the lever shown on the tree house?

5. On which side of the clearing can the squirrel be found? _____

Find the Deed

The Aldens' friends, the Andersons, would like to buy Broken Moon Pond. But someone is trying to stop them! Can you help find the missing deed to the property? Look for the letters **D-E-E-D** hidden in the office below.

Answers

Key Caper

Key #6 is the correct key.

Mmm-mmm, Good!

Possible words include:
ace, ape, cake, can, cap, cape, case, nap, nape, pace,
pack, pan, pea, peak, sac, sack, sake, sane, sank, sap,
scan, sea, snack, space, span

Canadian Crossword

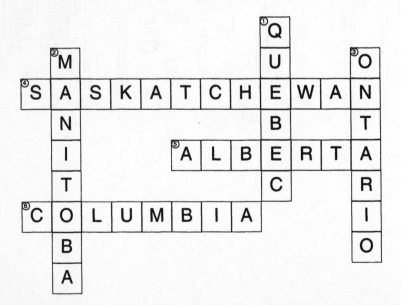

Field Journal Fun

Where's Orville?

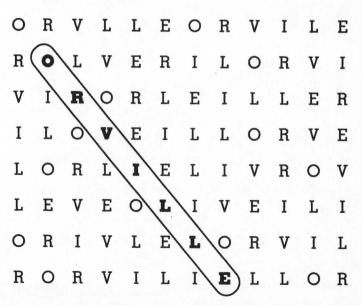

```
O   R   V   L   L   E   O   R   V   I   L   E

R   O   L   V   E   R   I   L   O   R   V   I

V   I   R   O   R   L   E   I   L   L   E   R

I   L   O   V   E   I   L   L   O   R   V   E

L   O   R   L   I   E   L   I   V   R   O   V

L   E   V   E   O   L   I   V   E   I   L   I

O   R   I   V   L   E   L   O   R   V   I   L

R   O   R   V   I   L   I   E   L   L   O   R
```

A Tasty Test

1. b
2. c
3. a

4. b
5. a
6. c

An A-maze-ing Tree House

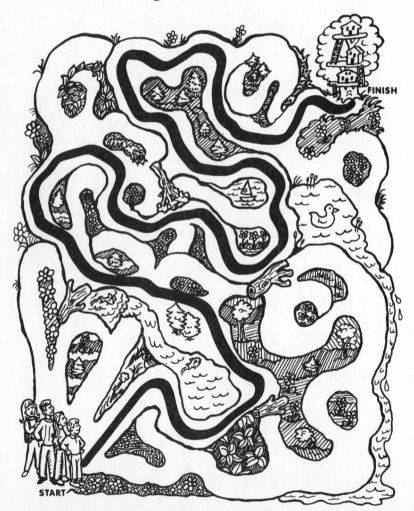

Do You Remember?

1. Zero
2. False
3. Eight
4.
5. The left side

Find the Deed

GERTRUDE CHANDLER WARNER discovered when she was teaching that many readers who like an exciting story could find no books that were both easy and fun to read. She decided to try to meet this need, and her first book, *The Boxcar Children*, quickly proved she had succeeded.

Miss Warner drew on her own experiences to write the mystery. As a child she spent hours watching trains go by on the tracks opposite her family home. She often dreamed about what it would be like to set up housekeeping in a caboose or freight car — the situation the Alden children find themselves in.

When Miss Warner received requests for more adventures involving Henry, Jessie, Violet, and Benny Alden, she began additional stories. In each, she chose a special setting and introduced unusual or eccentric characters who liked the unpredictable.

While the mystery element is central to each of Miss Warner's books, she never thought of them as strictly juvenile mysteries. She liked to stress the Aldens' independence and resourcefulness and their solid New England devotion to using up and making do. The Aldens go about most of their adventures with as little adult supervision as possible — something else that delights young readers.

Miss Warner lived in Putnam, Connecticut, until her death in 1979. During her lifetime, she received hundreds of letters from girls and boys telling her how much they liked her books.